TIMOTHY'S

A True Story

For Hugo, Penny and Giles

First published in Great Britain in Picture Lions 1992
Picture Lions is an imprint of the Children's Division,
part of HarperCollins Publishers Limited,
77-85 Fulham Palace Road, Hammersmith,
London W6 8JB

Copyright © Joanna Harrison 1992

A CIP catalogue record for this book
is available from the British Library.
The author asserts the moral right to
be identified as the author of the work.

ISBN: 0 00 664259-4

Printed and bound in Great Britain
by BPCC Paulton Books Ltd

This book is set in New Baskerville

TIMOTHY'S TEDDY

Joanna Harrison

PictureLions

An Imprint of HarperCollins Publishers

It was Christmas Eve. Tim had spent all afternoon
playing in the snow and now his toes were beginning
to get cold. Once inside the warm kitchen he quickly
took off his coat and boots and ran into the sitting room.

"There you are, Tim," said his mother who was decorating the Christmas tree, "come and have some tea and toast. You must be frozen!"

Tim took his toast and sat by the Christmas tree.
When he was sure no one was looking he squeezed
round the back of the tree to have a secret peek at
the presents. There he found the biggest parcel he'd
ever seen and it was for him. Whatever could it be...?

At last it was Christmas Day.
  Tim made himself useful handing out the presents until there was only one left...

"Happy Christmas!" said Tim's father as he handed him the huge parcel.

Tim carefully untied the ribbon and unwrapped the paper. Underneath was a big brown box. He opened the lid and peeped inside.

"Look !" shouted Tim as he pulled out an enormous teddy bear. "He's as big as me!"

Tim gave his new friend a hug then turned him upside down.

"Woargh" said Teddy.

"Wow!" said Tim.

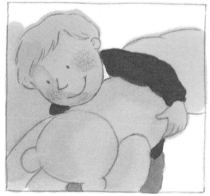

Tim proudly introduced Teddy to his family.
His daddy shook Teddy's hand, Mummy gave him
a cuddle and his little sister gave him a big kiss.
But Teddy was now Tim's friend, his best friend.
From then on Tim and Teddy were inseparable.
Everywhere Tim went Teddy went too.

That winter they went tobogganing.

In the spring they played cowboys and Indians.

One hot day in the summer, Tim thought Teddy might like to cool off in the paddling pool. His mother was not very pleased. Teddy spent the rest of the day hanging up to dry on the washing line.

In the autumn Teddy took a nasty fall off Tim's
tricycle and had to be brought back in the
wheelbarrow a little the worse for wear.

Sometimes Tim was so tired he'd forget to take Teddy to bed.

"Where's Teddy," he'd cry and the hunt would begin:

under the stairs; behind the sofa; up in the attic.
Then Tim would remember and all was well.

As Tim grew older, Teddy grew scruffier. But Tim didn't mind. Tim loved Teddy just as he was.

However, the day finally arrived when Tim was to go to school for the very first time.

When they arrived the teacher said, "I'm sorry Tim, your teddy can't stay. He's too big."

"Then I won't stay without Teddy, I won't!" cried Tim. But Tim had to stay and Teddy had to go home.

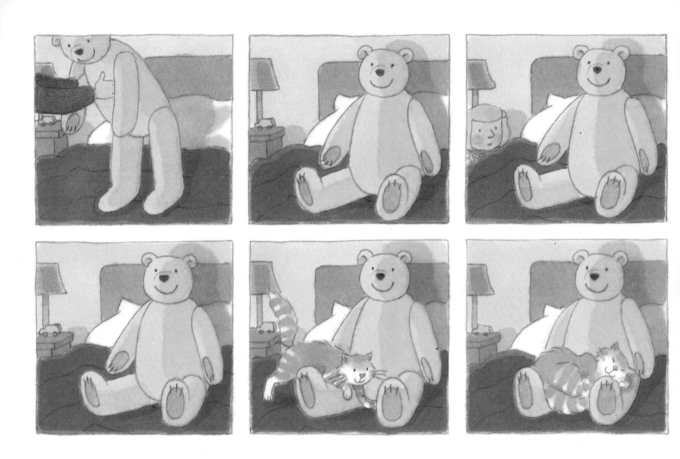

When Tim's mummy got back, she put Teddy on
Tim's bed. All day he waited for Tim to return.
At four o'clock, the door opened and Tim flung
himself on the bed.

"I wish you could have come to school with me
today," he said, giving Teddy a hug. "It was lots of fun!"

Days passed into weeks, and weeks into months.
Tim loved his school and soon made lots of friends.

One day Tim asked two boys from his class to come
and play at his home. Tim showed them his train set
and later on they played football in the garden. After
tea Tim said, "Let's go upstairs, there's someone I
want you to meet."

Tim ran into his bedroom and picked Teddy up.

"A teddy!" laughed one of his friends.

"How soppy," said the other.

Tim looked at Teddy. "Well, he's not really mine," he lied, and turning bright red he quickly shoved Teddy behind a chair.

"Don't you want Teddy?" said his mother that night when Tim was in bed.

"Oh no," said Tim. "I'm too old for teddies now."

Teddy never went back to Tim's room. He sat on the spare room bed for many months. Occasionally the cat would sleep on his lap. One day someone picked him up and put him in the attic.

Teddy sat in the dark. Mice would come and steal his straw stuffing, but Teddy didn't seem to care. One day the cat knocked him over and he fell out of sight behind a suitcase. No one noticed and he was soon forgotten about. Years passed...

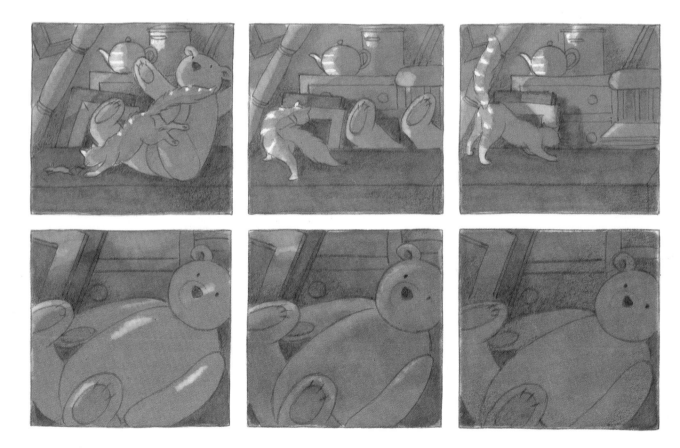

One day when Tim's sister, (who was by now quite grown up), was clearing out the attic, she found Teddy squashed behind a suitcase.

"Look!" she cried to her daughter, who was playing on the landing below. "It's Teddy! He used to be Uncle Tim's favourite teddy bear when he was a little boy."

"Poor old thing, I don't know if he's even worth keeping now."

She handed him to her daughter. "What do you think?"

"I think that he needs his fur brushing and something to eat, and just for tonight he can sleep in my bed."

But later that night Tim's sister took Teddy and sewed a new nose, two bright new eyes and a brand new smile onto Teddy's face. He now looked better than he had for years.

Then something awful happened. He was stuffed into a huge box and the lid was shut tightly above him.

Then the terrible journey began.

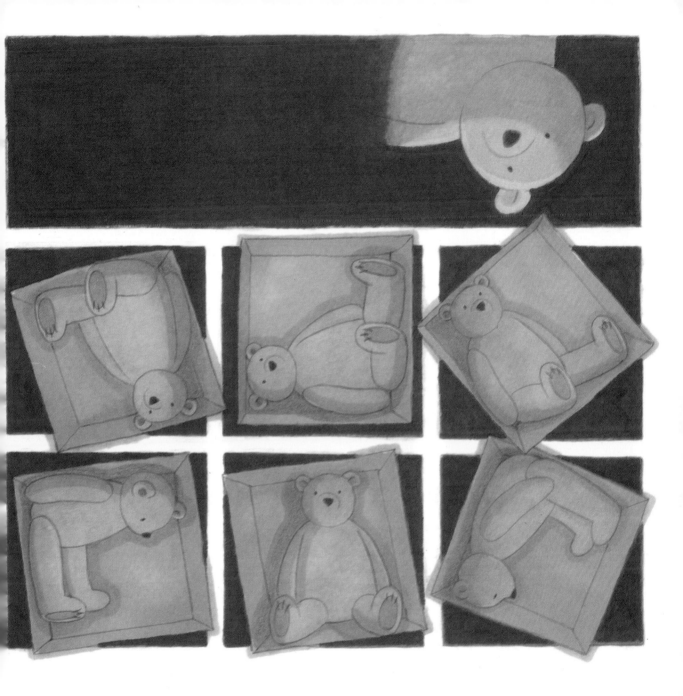

The noises were loud, there was a roaring like a lion's roar, that seemed to go on for ever. Teddy in his box was turned this way and that. It was cold and dark and frightening.

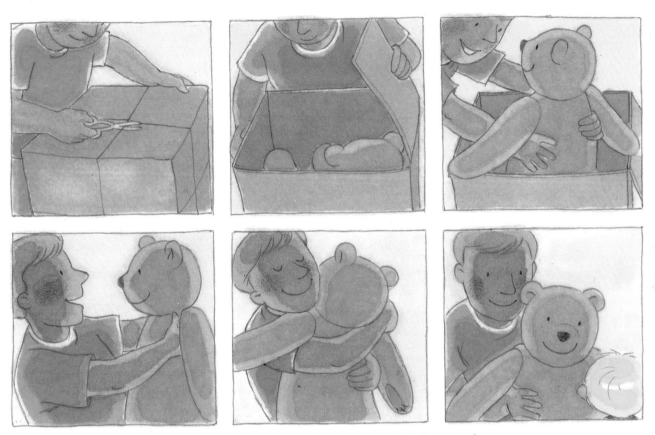

It was very hot and quiet when Teddy woke up. Suddenly the lid of the box opened and bright light flooded in.

As two hands pulled him out, Teddy looked up to see Tim, now grown up, but still the Tim he'd known.

"Daddy!" His little son tugged at his shirt. "Whose teddy is that?"

"He used to be mine when I was little," said Tim. "Now he's yours."

Giles loved his new teddy and everywhere that Giles went Teddy went too. They spent the next morning playing on the beach. It was very hot and sunny.
In the afternoon Tim took them to the zoo.

Before they went home, Tim stopped for a moment to show Giles and Teddy the sun setting over Sydney harbour. "Not a bad life for an old teddy," thought Tim happily.

THE END